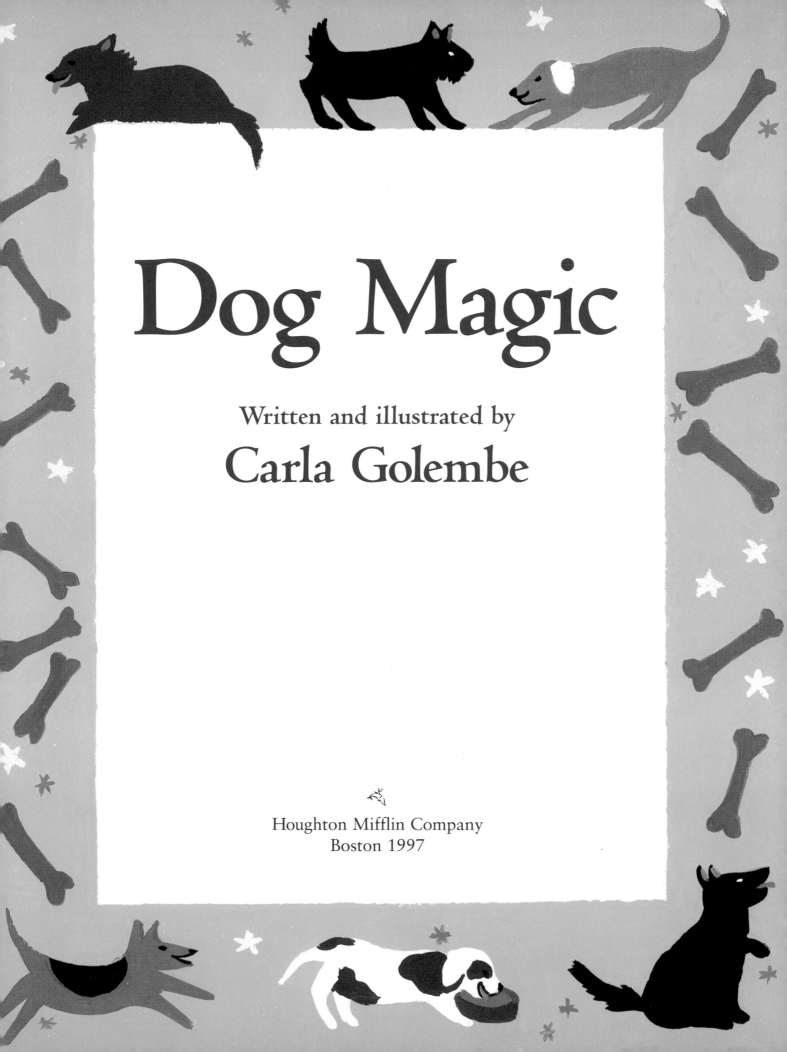

Dog Magic

Written and illustrated by

Carla Golembe

Houghton Mifflin Company
Boston 1997

For Robert Vargas, Kevin Almeroth, and Daisy, who inspired me;
my parents, who bought me my magic shoes;
Joe, who suggested I write about them;
and Ann Rider, for support and encouragement.

For information about this and other Houghton Mifflin trade and reference
books and multimedia products, visit The Bookstore at Houghton Mifflin
on the World Wide Web at http://www.hmco.com/trade/.

The text of this book is set in 16 point Sabon.
The illustrations are gouache, reproduced in full color.

Library of Congress Cataloging-in-Publication Data
Golembe, Carla.
Dog magic / written and illustrated by Carla Golembe.
p. cm.
Summary: Molly Gail loves all kinds of animals, but she is afraid of dogs — until,
on her seventh birthday, she gets such beautiful shoes that she forgets her fear.
ISBN 0-395-81662-9
1. Dogs — Fiction. 2. Fear — Fiction. I. Title. PZ7.G5814Do 1997
[E] — dc20 96-22235 CIP AC

Printed in the United States of America

HOR 10 9 8 7 6 5 4 3 2 1

Molly Gail lived in a house by the sea with her mother, father, and Willow the cat. "Molly Nightingale" her father liked to call her because Molly loved birds — pink birds, speckled birds, birds with green feathers, and birds with purple crests. She would sit on the porch and paint bright pictures of them. She loved fish and butterflies, too. And, of course, she loved cats. Molly Gail liked all the animals on earth except for one. She was afraid of dogs.

She was afraid of Daisy who lived with their neighbor, Mr. Vargas. Daisy was huge and had a long pink tongue. She'd lick people all over their faces. Mr. Vargas said she was just kissing them but it looked creepy to Molly.

She was afraid of Chiche who slept in the corner of Midge's fruit stand.

Chiche had the sharpest, whitest teeth Molly had ever seen.

And she was especially afraid of Paris who liked to jump up on people.

Paris never seemed to stand still.

On her seventh birthday Molly's parents gave her a box tied with a great purple bow. "Hot bananas!" Molly cried when she opened the box and lifted out a pair of shoes.

They were turquoise and had purple bows and pink and yellow stars. "Magic shoes," she named them and put them on. They fit perfectly.

The next day Molly wore her new shoes to school. All day her steps were as light as pink flamingoes. After she had walked home from school she realized something very strange. She had passed two dogs on the way and both times she had forgotten to be afraid! She hadn't ducked behind a tree, her hands hadn't started

sweating or her knees shaking. That night she said to her family,
"I think my magic shoes must really *be* magic. When I wear them,
I'm not afraid of dogs."

"Well maybe now you can be friends with them," her mother suggested.

"Maybe I can," said Molly thoughtfully.

Early Saturday morning Molly put on her magic shoes. Today, she decided, she would not hide or run away if she saw a dog. She would just walk calmly by. No sooner had Molly Gail turned the corner by her house when she saw a huge white dog with black spots running down the street straight toward her. It was Paris!

Molly looked down at her shoes. "Make me as brave, magic shoes," she whispered, "as brave as a palm tree in a storm!" When Molly looked up Paris was right in front of her.

"Hello, Paris," she said quietly.

Paris wagged his tail.

Very slowly, Molly reached out to touch the dog's head.

Gently she patted his soft fur. Paris wagged his tail a little harder.

"You aren't going to jump up on me, are you, Paris?"

Paris kept wagging his tail but not once did he jump up. Then he started running in a little circle around Molly. Faster and faster he ran, but this time Molly wasn't scared — she thought Paris looked funny, like a whirling, blurring black and white pinwheel. She laughed and Paris barked back.

After that day Molly Gail became friends with all the dogs in her neighborhood — tall dogs, little dogs, furry dogs, dogs with pointy ears,

and dogs with floppy ears. Her parents, and even Willow, got used to finding dogs sitting on the porch waiting for Molly to play with them.

Molly Gail began to draw pictures of dogs in school. She painted a portrait of Daisy with her big pink tongue hanging out. She painted Paris jumping high in the air.

And she made a picture of Chiche with her bright pointy-tooth smile which Midge hung over the pineapples.

Everyone liked Molly's pictures so much that her teachers asked her to show them at school on parents' night.

All the dogs came. Molly wore her favorite dress and, of course, her magic shoes.

Then one day, the day before her eighth birthday, Molly put on her
shoes and they didn't fit. They were so tight that they hurt her feet.
"We'll see what we can do, Molly," her mother told her. "But for now
you'll have to wear your sneakers."

So, Molly put on her sneakers. She went outside and began walking slowly. Already her knees were shaking. What would the dogs do now that she wasn't wearing her magic shoes? One by one they came to meet her.

Daisy came first. Molly stopped walking as soon as she saw her. But Daisy kept trotting toward her with her big pink tongue hanging out. Then came Chiche, grinning her toothy grin. Paris

started running around her in circles, and Molly couldn't help laughing.

She knelt down to hug each one of them. "You dogs," she said, "are my magic dogs."

The next morning Molly Gail's parents gave her a big box for her eighth birthday. There were small holes in it. She untied the ribbon and lifted the lid. A little yellow face with black eyes and a wet nose looked out at her.

"Hot bananas!" Molly cried.

Molly Gail and the puppy looked at each other. "You wonderful magical puppy," she said. "I will call you Magic."

Molly brought Magic to meet the other dogs. And from that day on they were all very good friends. Paris showed Magic how to run in circles and make children laugh. Chiche taught him how to smile

in such a way that everyone would want to give him belly rubs. And
Daisy showed him how to lick children's faces, but very gently, so as
not to scare them.

At home in the house by the sea, Magic had his place on the porch with Molly and Willow. And when Molly grew up, she became an artist and made a book about him and the other magic dogs. This is it.